Please Don't
Ask Me
to Love You

by
Anne Schraff

Perfection Learning Corporation
Logan, Iowa 51546

Cover: Doug Knutson

1 TINA HAYES ALWAYS told the boys she dated that she had to be home early because her mother was very strict. That wasn't the case at all. Her mother wasn't strict.

Tonight Tina gave the same excuse. Jimmy didn't seem too happy about it, but he agreed to take her home.

Going home and getting in the door was another problem. Tina never let any of her dates near her house. She never knew what would be happening inside. But whatever it was, it would probably be something that would embarrass her.

As usual, when the car stopped in front of her house, Tina got out as quickly as possible.

"I had a lot of fun, Jimmy," she said.

"The movie was great, wasn't it?" Jimmy said.

"Great," Tina said, trying to close the door before he offered to go in with her. "Thanks. See you, huh?"

She made it. She ran halfway up the walk before turning and waving goodbye.

She felt greatly relieved when Jimmy

waved back and drove off. Already she could hear voices coming from inside her house. The voices were loud. Tina could tell that her mother was arguing with a man. Tina hoped it wasn't Harry.

"Let it be anyone but Harry," she whispered. Her hands shook as she opened the door.

"What's she doing home?" Harry yelled as soon as he saw her. "You said the kid wouldn't be home tonight."

Tina looked quickly to her mother for help. But she could see that her mother wasn't going to stick up for her. Her mother was only thirty-three years old, and she used to be beautiful. But tonight she looked old. Tina could tell that her mother was too tired to protect her from Harry.

"What happened, sweetie?" Tina's mother asked, ignoring Harry's question and Tina's silent plea for help. "Why are you home so early? Was your date a dud?"

"It's almost midnight, Mom," Tina explained.

"So what?" Harry grumbled. "You turn into a pumpkin or something at midnight?"

Tina didn't feel like fighting with Harry, so she kept her mouth shut. It was never a smart idea to fight with Harry anyway. He was a tall, heavy-set man. He looked mean.

Harry seemed to like Tina's mother— they'd been dating off and on for a couple of months. But he'd always hated Tina.

"Mom, you said I should be home by midnight, remember?" Tina said.

"Did I?" her mother said. "I forgot." She turned toward Harry and smiled. "You quit picking on her. Okay, honey?"

"I want her out of here!" Harry hollered.

Tina looked at her mother, but her mother was pouring herself a drink.

"It's too late to go out again," Tina stammered. If she could just get to her bedroom and lock herself in. Then maybe Harry would leave her alone.

Tina turned to run for it, but Harry was

quick. He stopped her with his fist, hitting her hard in the face. She fell back, knocking over the coffee table and breaking a vase.

Tina lay stunned on the floor. She felt as if her head were exploding. Her face was on fire with pain and shame. She could feel her left eye swelling up quickly.

"Mom!" she cried weakly.

Tina's mother had not even seen what happened. Her back had been turned as she put fresh ice in her drink. Now when Tina called out, she turned slowly. She looked with surprise at Tina. Her pretty eyes widened. She stared down at Tina with the empty gaze of a doll.

Tina struggled to her feet. Then, grabbing her big straw bag, she ran to the front door and let herself out. The cold night air of Albuquerque slapped at her face as she fled down the sidewalk. Her mind was spinning and her head throbbed.

Most of the houses on the street were dark. Then Tina spotted a light at the Hadley house further down the block. She baby-sat for the two little Hadley girls sometimes. Maybe the Hadleys would help her.

Tina hurried to the Hadley house. She started to knock, but couldn't do it. If she told the Hadleys what really happened, then her mother would get in trouble. The Hadleys would call the police, and the police would find Tina's mother drinking with Harry. Harry would be arrested for hitting Tina. Tina's mother might be arrested, too. And Tina would end up in juvenile hall with a bunch of tough kids.

Tina turned and walked down the dark street. She looked around desperately. She couldn't go back home. Harry would just beat her up. And she didn't have any close friends who would help her.

No close relatives, either. Tina had an aunt who lived two thousand miles away and hardly knew her. That wasn't any help. She had nowhere to go.

Then she remembered a girl from school talking about an empty building behind a motorcycle shop. The girl had said kids could hang out there. Nobody bothered them. Sometimes there would be free food, too. Tina knew where the place was.

Tina stopped under a street light and looked in her bag. She had twenty dollars. She always kept her baby-sitting money in her bag. It wasn't safe to leave it in the house with people like Harry around.

She closed her bag and headed for the bike shop. Her left eye was almost swollen shut now and her whole head ached. She just wanted to lie down someplace where it was quiet.

Tina wondered what she would do on Monday. She had a biology test to take. She was bad enough in biology with two good eyes.

Then she wondered what the other kids would say about her black eye. And the teachers—what would they think? Maybe they'd get suspicious. Especially Ms. Bronson. She was always suspicious anyway. She might call the authorities to investigate. Tina shuddered at that thought.

For the first time in her life, Tina

thought about quitting school. She'd always planned to graduate and get a decent job. But suddenly going back to school seemed impossible. How could she cope with all the questions and those silent suspicions?

The image of her locker drifted into her mind. She wondered just what happened to the lockers of students who never returned. Would her old number 718 just sit there gathering dust? What would they do with her pictures and notebooks?

As Tina turned over these questions, she reached the bike shop and saw the empty building next to it. The building looked tightly locked. But she could see some people moving around in the field beyond the building. They were talking in soft, muffled voices.

Scrawny trees and bushes stood around the field. The trees looked as weak and lonely as the people she saw standing near them.

Making her way toward the group, Tina almost stumbled over a boy. He was lying in a sleeping bag right in the middle of the field.

Then another voice called, "Hi."

Tina turned to stare at the young man who had greeted her. She hoped it was somebody from school, but it wasn't.

"Hi," she said. "Say, is that empty building over there the one where people can, uh—stay?"

"They boarded it up. There's just the field now. You looking for somebody special?"

Tina shook her head.

"I don't know anybody here either," he said. "My name is Jack."

"I'm Tina."

"I got a little fire over there. I'm heating some bean soup. Come on over," Jack said.

Tina went to the fire and sat down across from Jack.

"You here for the first time, Tina?"

"Yeah."

"You running away from somebody?"

"I guess so," Tina admitted.

"That's okay. We're all running away from somebody."

He studied her for a moment. Then he said. "That's a nasty bruise. Did your boyfriend hit you?"

"No. My mom's boyfriend did," Tina said.

Jack smiled. "Your boyfriend should have beaten him up."

"I don't have a boyfriend."

Jack smiled more. "Well, well. I don't have a girlfriend. Maybe we met at the right time." He laughed.

"Look, I just want to lie down and sleep. My head hurts something awful," Tina said.

"Listen, Tina. I've got a motorcycle. I won't be sticking around here long. I wouldn't mind taking you with me when I go. I do construction work—make pretty good money at it. You could do worse, Tina." Jack leaned forward and took Tina's hand.

Tina felt very uncomfortable. "Thanks, but I don't want to go anyplace. I mean, I'm only sixteen and I'm in high school and maybe—well, maybe things will be okay at home in the morning."

Jack didn't let go of Tina's hand. "Aw, come on. You won't go home again. I can see it in your face."

Now Tina felt frightened. Jack was holding her hand too tightly. "Please, Jack. I just want to rest now. Okay?"

"Tina, stick with me. You won't be sorry. Come on. Look, Tina, the world is a rough place. Lot of crummy people around. You should see the rotten people right around here—man, they'll tear you to pieces. You need somebody to protect you. If you think you're hurting now, just think what'll happen if you stick around here with no one to look out for you."

Tina pulled on her hand, but Jack's grip was too tight. The top of her head began to burn. "Please let go of me. I feel awful. My head hurts bad."

He got angry. "Don't pull that 'innocent little girl' bit on me. I can tell that you're a tough kid. I'll bet it was your boyfriend who did beat you up. And you probably dropped out of high school a long time ago. I know your type. You can't fool me. You and me belong together."

Tina jerked her arm away and jumped up. But Jack did the same. He glared at her, his eyes burning like hot coals.

"Oh, you want to fight, huh?" He laughed savagely. "That's okay with me!"

Jack started towards her. Tina stumbled backward, numb with fear.

2 THE SAUCEPAN BUBBLING with bean soup caught Tina's eye. She stooped and grabbed it, hurling the contents at Jack. He let out a long scream and staggered. Tina kicked him in the shins, turned, and began to run. She didn't know where she was running to, but she knew she had to keep going.

Tina spied a van parked farther down the street. She could hear a man's voice coming from it. He was singing in a twangy country voice,

Thank you, Lord, for legs to stroll,
and thank you, Lord, for eyes to see,
and thank you, Lord, for mockingbirds,
who give their sweet, sweet song to me.

But Tina wasn't really listening to the words. She was too frightened by the sound of footsteps behind her. She glanced back long enough to see Jack gaining on her. He looked mad. The bean soup had been really hot and had burned his face.

The singing could still be heard from

the van.

Thank you, Lord, for ears to hear,
and thank you, Lord, for a voice to sing,
and thank you, Lord, for all my friends,
who never try to tie down my wings.

Tina reached the van and pounded on the doors. "Help me!" she cried, and the singing stopped. The door opened and a young man stood there looking at Tina. He was holding a guitar.

Jack stopped a few yards back. He was panting hard and his face was twisted in fury. He looked at the guitar man and said, "Just stay out of this, mister, if you know what's good for you. That girl threw hot soup in my face for no reason, and I'm going to teach her a little lesson. So just get back inside that van."

The guitar man thoughtfully shook his head and looked at Tina. "Did you do that?" he asked in a southern drawl.

Tina thought fast. She had to make the guitar man believe that Jack was dangerous. "Look what he did to my face!"

The guitar man whistled. "Shouldn't have done that, mister."

"She's a liar!" Jack shouted. "Some other guy did that. Now just stay out of this!"

Suddenly the guitar man had a knife in his hand. Its long, sharp blade winked in the street light. "Git!" he snapped at Jack.

There was so much savagery in his voice that Jack didn't argue. He turned and hurried away.

The guitar man turned the knife and examined the blade for a moment. Then he laughed. "I never stuck nobody with this, but I scared a few off." He calmly put the knife away.

Tina finally took a breath. "Thanks."

"Don't mention it. You best git on home now, Susie. You don't look much more than junior high, and this sure isn't a nice place for a young girl."

"My name isn't Susie, it's Tina. And I'm sixteen and I can't go home," Tina said.

"That's quite a mouthful," the guitar man commented.

Now that her fear had passed, Tina really studied him for the first time. He was young—about twenty. His thick hair and eyes were the same shade of brown. He had good features, but he was too skinny. Though he was dressed in old clothes—a cracked leather jacket and worn jeans—he was neat and clean.

"You sure can't stay around here," he said. "Not unless you're crazy. Or maybe you want to run after that guy I just chased off."

Tina didn't know why, but she trusted the guitar man. He seemed nice and decent. She desperately needed someone's company for a little while. Someone who wouldn't hit or hurt her.

"I don't know where to go," she finally said.

"Then call a cop."

"They'd throw me in juvenile hall."

"I'm sorry." He started to go back inside the van. He stopped then, but he didn't say anything.

"What's your name?" Tina asked him.

"Piney Woods."

"No kidding?"

"No kidding."

Tina forced the words out. "Would you let me hitch a ride with you for just a little way? I'm so tired. I wouldn't bother you. I'd just sleep in a corner and then get out."

Piney laughed. "Come on, Susie, I don't need that kind of trouble. A kid like you? You must be nuts. I'm going to the desert north of Los Angeles. You wouldn't find anything there."

"You could drop me off in L.A.," Tina said.

"I'm no fool, Susie."

"My name isn't Susie. And I've got twenty dollars. I'll pay you if you take me to L.A."

"Get a taxi," he said.

"Hey, wait," Tina yelled when he started to close the door again. "I'm—look, I'm *scared*!"

He closed the door.

Tina screamed at the closed van. She

thought of every curse she'd ever heard and yelled them all into the cold, dark night. Then she shouted, "I hope you hit a chuckhole and bust that stupid van of yours!" Tears streamed down her hot, swollen face.

Suddenly the door opened again. Piney stood there, staring angrily at her. He didn't say anything for a minute. Then he snapped, "Okay. Just to L.A. That's all."

Tina climbed into the van. "I won't be any bother."

"I'm not betting on that," he said angrily.

Tina curled up in one corner while he climbed behind the wheel. In another minute, the van was in motion. Tina was so tired she fell asleep in two minutes.

A jolt of the van woke her up hours later. She sat up. Her tears were now dry, but her skin felt strange and swollen. Her black eye ached.

All her misery and fear washed over her again. She couldn't believe what was happening to her. She'd run away. Maybe she would never see her home or her mother again.

She thought about her warm, comfortable bedroom. In her mind, she saw the patchwork quilt on the bed. She'd made it herself.

"Mom!" Tina softly cried. A longing to see her mother swept over her. She wanted to explain that running away had been a mistake. It was just that Harry had hurt her.

Maybe it wasn't too late, she thought. She called out to Piney, "Where are we?"

Piney turned his head towards her for a second. "Finally up, are you? Well, we're about three hours from The City of Industry."

"Can we stop at a gas station or something? I have to call my mother," Tina said.

"Next exit," he said. He seemed calmer—almost happy.

He took the next off-ramp. As they pulled up, Tina glanced at a clock in the station. It was six in the morning.

Piney sat in the van with the engine

running while Tina ran to the phone booth.

Tina's hands shook as she dialed. She would tell her mother she was coming right home. Her mother must be worried sick by now. She was probably blaming herself for what had happened.

Sometimes when her mother drank too much, she'd start blaming herself. When she got in one of those moods, she always said the same things. Tina knew the speech by heart. Her mother would say she was sorry she wasn't a better mother. And Tina would say what she always said, "Oh, Mom. Please don't say that. I need you." Then everything would be okay—at least for a while.

The phone rang for a long time. When somebody finally answered, it was Harry.

"I want to talk to my mother," Tina said.

Harry swore.

"Put my mother on!" Tina shouted. Tina heard a woman laughing in the background. It had to be her mother.

Tina's heart sank. Her mother must have had a lot to drink last night. She probably didn't even know Tina was gone. Usually when she drank a lot, she didn't remember much of anything. In fact, that's why she did it: she drank to forget.

Tina begged Harry, "Please, let me talk to her."

For answer, Harry slammed the receiver in Tina's ear.

"My mother wasn't home," Tina told Piney when she got back to the van. He looked disappointed.

They continued driving north. After awhile, Piney started singing again.

Cry if you want to, and laugh if you can.
Smile in the mirror, or dance in the sand.
Do what you want to, or do what you should,
Do whatever your heart says is good.

Tina listened to the song in silence. Then when he finished, she asked, "Do you have a mother, Piney?"

"Nope. Once did."

"Do you have anybody?"

"Not a living soul this side of heaven, Susie."

Tina looked out the window of the van to the east. The sun was coming up like a red fire. Slowly the sun's bright rays pushed back the darkness.

In an hour, the whole sky was blue. Piney glanced at Tina and said, "Breakfast time. You hungry?"

Tina nodded.

A few minutes later, Piney pulled into a hillside campground. In a short time he had hotcakes made. He passed a heaping plate to Tina and she dug in quickly.

"What do you do for a living?" Tina asked Piney between bites.

"Sing songs."

"You mean for pay?" Tina was surprised.

He grinned. "Do I sound *that* bad?"

"No. I just never met anybody who made their living singing before."

"I'm able to land gigs about every other night. I'm not getting rich, but it's enough to see me through."

He looked at Tina then, his face serious. "We'll stop at a gas station and call your mama. I expect she's home by now."

Tina felt a lump in her throat. She stared at her plate. "I don't think I can go home."

"Aw, shoot, why not?"

"I just can't." Tina looked up at Piney. "See, my mother has a boyfriend. He hates me."

"Is he the one who hit you?" Piney guessed. "It wasn't that punk after all?"

"Yeah."

"Your mama let him do it?"

"She—" But Tina couldn't be disloyal to her mother, even now. She wasn't going to tell a perfect stranger about her mother or their problems. "She's sick, you see. She has this sickness and she doesn't always know what's going on."

Piney grunted and then got up, gathering the pan and plates. They got in the van and drove to a gas station down the road. Piney said, "You call your mother now and tell her you're coming home."

Tina went to the pay phone and dialed her home again. It was eight in the morning. The phone rang and rang.

Finally her mother answered. She sounded sick. "Who is this? You woke me up."

"It's Tina. Mom—I'm sorry I ran away like that. I just got scared. So I hitched a ride with a guy. I guess I'd better come home, huh?"

Tina's mother didn't seem to have heard. She said, "Oh, Tina. Honey, I've got some news for you. Harry said he was going to marry me. Isn't that something? Harry said we can get the license today."

"Mom," Tina begged, "tell me what to do." She started to cry.

"I never thought he'd want to marry me," her mother went on. "We're going for the license today."

She paused and finally seemed to catch up with what Tina had said. "Now what were you saying, baby? About hitching a ride? Well, honey, don't worry about coming home right away if you're having a good time. No, don't you worry about coming home.''

Tina closed her eyes, but the tears slipped through anyway. She remembered something her mother had said once, long ago:

I guess I was never meant to be a mother, baby. I never wanted to be a mother. I tried to love you. God knows I tried.

"Goodbye, Mama," Tina said softly. She hung up the phone and stared out of the phone booth. She saw Piney standing outside the van. He was leaning against the closed door, looking impatient.

Tina knew he didn't want her either. But he was all she had left. She didn't have a home anymore.

3 TINA WALKED SLOWLY back to the van. Piney immediately asked her the question she'd been dreading. "Your mother going to come for you?"

"No," Tina said. Then she blurted out, "She doesn't want me to come home at all."

He looked confused. "Can't be," he said.

Tina straightened her shoulders. "Look, if you can break my twenty, I'll pay you for dropping me off in L.A."

Piney's eyes narrowed. "What are you going to do in L.A.?"

"What's it to you?" Tina demanded.

"Hey, listen, what kind of a job are they going to give a scrawny kid like you? A *decent* job, that is."

Tina felt both ashamed and irritated. "I'll be a waitress. Anybody can do that."

"You think they want a fifteen-year-old runaway waiting on tables, Susie?"

"My name's not Susie, and I'm sixteen! And mind your own business!" Tina snapped.

"Only thing you're going to find is trouble."

Tina glared at Piney. "Don't act like you care, because you don't. Nobody does."

"Little runty kid pushes herself on me—Well, I guess I'm involved whether I want to be or not," Piney said.

"Just forget about me!" Tina said.

"Okay, okay. Have it your way. Let's get started. I want to be in L.A. before tonight."

They drove north and eventually reached the outskirts of Los Angeles. Tina saw a smokestack spitting fire into the air south of the city. She also noticed the stream of traffic thicken. She stared as the cars sped past, each one filled with grim-looking strangers.

Her stomach tightened with fear. Everybody was a stranger; everything seemed so threatening. She felt like she was drowning in a swirling river of cars and smoke.

"You sure you want me to drop you in L.A., Susie?" Piney asked after a while.

"I could just as easy take you to the Antelope Valley. I got a gig in a little place called The Century Plant. They'd let you wash dishes for your keep. You could stay in the van for a while. No sweat."

Tina licked her dry lips. "Well—well, maybe."

Los Angeles came and went, a blur of blue-gray smoke. A few skyscrapers poked their heads out of the smoggy sky. They seemed to be searching for something.

And then the world turned green as they drove through the San Fernando Valley. This passed, too, as they drove into a region of dry hills. Craggy rocks, red with iron, filled the landscape. It looked like the moon.

They passed through a medium-size city and Piney headed down a side street. He pulled up in front of a roadside bar. "There she is," he announced. "The Century Plant."

Tina peered at the bar. "It looks kind of tough."

Piney smiled. "Well, it's not fancy."

"You sure it's okay if I just hang around for a while?" Tina asked him. "I mean, why should you be doing this for me? Nobody does something for nothing."

Piney looked at Tina. "Just what do you think I want?"

Tina felt embarrassed. She knew what men usually expected of her mother. She'd seen that too often.

"I don't know. And I really don't know you. You might be even worse than that guy who was chasing me last night."

Piney laughed. "That's right. I'm an escaped murderer."

"Don't make jokes. I just want you to understand that I only want to hang around for a little while. I'll be going home soon. My mom's getting better."

"She drinks, doesn't she?" Piney abruptly said.

Tina turned on him. "What if she does? That's a sickness!"

"Cool down, Susie. You ain't the only one hurting. My parents died of that sickness. Daddy was driving a truck. Only he wasn't fit to drive. Both of my parents died in the accident."

Tina said nothing. She looked away.

Piney sighed and got out of the van. Tina got out, too, and followed him into The Century Plant.

It was cool and dark inside. But not much else about the bar was to Tina's taste. The place smelled of beer, fried potatoes, and stale grease.

A fat, bearded man approached them and grabbed Piney's hand. "Hey, Piney boy! You sure are a sight for sore eyes!" he exclaimed.

"Hey, Tuba," Piney grinned. "You being a good ol' boy?"

"You bet." Tuba shifted his gaze to Tina. "Well, who's this?"

"My sister," Piney said.

The fat man winked. "Another sister, huh, Piney? You sure got a lot of sisters!"

When Tuba left to wait on a customer, Tina said, "You got a lot of girlfriends, huh?"

"A few. That ruffle your feathers?"

"Of course not. Why should it?" Tina said.

Yet Tina couldn't deny to herself that she sort of liked Piney Woods. He'd been kind to her even when she'd been nasty to him.

But she knew that Piney thought of her as a pesty kid. Never in a million years would a guy as nice as he was be interested in a girl like her.

For the rest of the day, Piney practiced and chatted with old acquaintances. Tina explored a little of the city on foot, but she mostly stayed close to The Century Plant. In payment for her food, she helped out in the kitchen. Tuba even paid her a little extra for her work.

That night, Piney rigged a curtain in the van. It divided the vehicle into two: one side for Tina and one side for him.

Before Piney went to sleep he played his guitar and sang a little. His voice softly sifted through the curtain.

Never knew a man to turn down clean cash.

Never knew a man to pick a sorry fight.
But I've known men who'd run like
    fools
through headstrong wind and hills of
    snow,
through fire blazing red-hot hot,
all for a kiss from a pretty girl.

Brother, you ain't known nothing yet,
you ain't seen a blessed thing,
you ain't tasted heaven's own dew,
till you had a kiss from a pretty girl.

He stopped singing then and soon Tina heard him breathing evenly. He was asleep.

Tina pulled the blanket tighter and thought about Piney. She couldn't quite believe that he was helping her out just because he was a decent person.

Yet Piney wasn't like the men her mother dated. Her mother's boyfriends were rough. None of them liked Tina. Some like Harry had even hurt her. The problem was they wanted Tina's mother all to themselves, and they forced her mother to choose.

Then Tina admitted the painful truth to herself. Sometimes the jealous boyfriends didn't even have to force her mother to choose. She seemed to resent having Tina around.

Tina had simply learned to stay out of the way when her mother had a boyfriend over. Usually they drank too much, and sometimes Tina's mother would get mad. Once in a while she would get so mad that she would hit Tina.

Afterwards her mother would be very sorry for having hurt Tina. Then she would be extra nice for the next few days. She would say over and over, "I'm sorry, sweetie. I'm so sorry. I didn't mean to hurt you. I love you. You know that, don't you?" And everything would be all right—for a while.

Tina knew her mother loved her, and Tina wanted to please her. Besides, Tina thought, it was easy to forgive her when she couldn't help acting that way.

Finally Tina fell asleep. But even in her sleep she couldn't escape her past. She dreamed about a time when she had run away once before. She'd been just ten years old then, and she'd gone no farther than the neighbor's garage. She'd hidden all night and gone home the next morning.

She found her mother waiting up for her. She'd seemed both relieved and angry to see Tina.

After Tina explained, her mother began asking strange questions. "Have you been telling lies about about me to anyone, Tina?"

"No."

"Do you ever tell people I hurt you?"

"No, Mama." It was true. Tina never told anybody about her mother.

"Do you know what will happen if you tell people bad things about me, Tina?" her mother asked. She didn't wait for Tina to answer. "I'll tell you what'll happen. They'll put me in jail. They'll put you in a terrible place, too. And we'll never see each other again."

Tina had sobbed wildly at that grim warning.

And now, in her sleep, Tina sobbed

again.

She heard a voice calling her. "Hey, Susie! Susie!"

Tina opened her eyes. She saw Piney looming over her in the dark. His face looked as wild as Jack's had.

"Get away from me!" Tina lashed out at him. So he was like all the rest after all! "Just get away!"

4 PINEY QUICKLY DREW back. Tina immediately realized how wrong she was. She felt like such a fool.

"You were crying. I thought you were sick," Piney explained. His eyes were filled with hurt.

"I was having a stupid nightmare," Tina said.

Piney went back to his side of the van. Tina was ashamed of herself. She hadn't wanted to hurt him. It was just that experience had taught her very few people can be trusted.

Neither Piney nor Tina mentioned the incident the next day. Both seemed eager to put it behind them. Besides, Piney was busying preparing for his show. Tina was amazed to see many signs throughout the city—including a big one outside the bar—advertising Piney's show.

"They've really got signs with your name on it," she said.

He laughed. "I got a big following. I'll have fans coming all the way from Canoga Park to see me tonight."

"Yeah?"

"You bet. Good folks from Arkansas and Alabama and Oklahoma. They've been in California a long time. They're homesick for good country music. They even come from Bakersfield to hear me. And they've got fine country music there."

That night, Piney looked confident when he stepped out onto the little stage. He really looked handsome, too, in his outfit. He wore black pants, a black coat with embroidery on the sleeves, and a red satin shirt. Tina couldn't believe how good he looked.

Tina had worked all day helping Tuba's wife with the cooking and cleaning. Now she sat at a table and watched Piney. Just as he had said, a lot of people had come. When they saw Piney, they called out his name. Some of the women threw him kisses.

When Piney began to sing, he sounded different, too.

Ask me to cover your loneliness,

ask me to shelter your dreams,
but please don't ask me to love you,
that's something I just can't do.

His voice was richer and nicer from up there on the stage. Tina couldn't take her eyes off him.

Ask me for smiles when you're sad,
ask me for songs when you're blue,
but please don't ask me to stay.
You can't change my traveling ways.

Like the sun that's here for a season,
like the dark that covers the day,
I can't stay long, I just sing my song,
then like sweet innocence I'm gone.

"Ain't that beautiful?" a woman sitting next to Tina said.

"Yeah," Tina said. And it *was* beautiful. In some crazy way it was. It was painful, too. It was as though Piney Woods was singing just for Tina. He was singing the words that everybody said to her. Because she felt like nobody had ever loved her—not even her mother.

"He's going to be another Randy Travis or Hank Williams, Jr.," the woman said. "You mark my words." She looked closer at Tina then. "Do you know him?"

"Yeah."

The woman smiled. "Hey, do you think you could get his autograph for me? I'd sure be obliged."

"Okay," Tina said. In the next break between songs, she walked up to the stage. "Lady over there wants your autograph," she said and shoved the pad at him.

He grinned. "No kidding?"

"No kidding. She thinks you're another Hank Williams, Jr., or somebody." Tina looked down as she spoke. "You *are* kind of good."

"Are you putting me on?"

"No. You sound great on the stage." Tina took the autograph back to the woman.

When Tina sat down again, a young, well-dressed man leaned toward her.

"Excuse me. Do you know the fella singing?"

Tina nodded. "He's, uh—my brother."

"Is that right?" The young man smiled. He was handsome and obviously rich. "My name is Arthur Morley. My folks run a quarter horse ranch in Chatsworth."

"I'm Tina—Tina Woods," she lied.

"Your brother sings very well. I'm a country music fan."

Tina was wearing dark glasses to hide her black eye. But she felt self-conscious anyway. She was wearing a simple shirt and jeans, and she thought she must look terrible.

"Do you sing, too?" Arthur asked Tina.

"Oh, no. My brother has all the talent in the family." Tina found herself saying things before she even thought.

"Well, you weren't shortchanged in looks, Tina," Arthur said.

Tina blushed.

"I bet you're even prettier without those glasses."

"I—I'm wearing them because I've got

a black eye. I'm so clumsy sometimes."
Tina tried to laugh. But it hurt her face
when she laughed.

"This is a nice little place," Arthur said.
"I've seen a lot of young country singers
start in stands like this. Your brother
looks to me like he's going places."

"I hope so."

"Just the two of you in town?" he
asked.

"Yeah. Piney and me, we decided to
just head out and try life on our own,"
Tina said.

Arthur Morley looked like the kind of
guy who wouldn't understand poverty.
So Tina decided to make her background
sound better. "Our folks have a big ranch
in Arkansas. They wanted us to go to college and stuff."

"My folks are the same way," Arthur
smiled. "But our generation has to find
its own way, don't you think?"

"Yeah, sure," Tina said.

"Seems like we have a lot in common,
Tina," Arthur said, scooting his chair
closer. "How old are you?"

"I'm—eighteen," Tina said quickly.

"I'm twenty," he said. "I'm in college right now, but I don't like it much."

"My mother taught English before she was married," Tina added. The lies came easily now. "My mother is smart."

"Tina, would I be coming on too strong if I asked you out?" Arthur smiled in a charming way and put his hand on Tina's arm.

Tina smiled, too. Arthur was such a classy guy. Tina had never dated someone like him. All the boys who had asked her out had been kind of cheap and grabby. Tina figured that was because all the nice boys knew about her problems at home.

"Sure, that would be fun," Tina said.

After Arthur left, Tina felt guilty. She'd told him so many lies. She'd built a complete fairy tale.

But the lies had to be better than the truth. Tina believed that if she'd told Arthur that she was really a sixteen-year-old runaway with a mother who drinks, he would have fled in the other direction.

And Tina didn't want that to happen. She wanted to prove to herself that a nice guy would ask her out. She was so used to feeling like a pest—like something to be stepped on. And usually that's what happened: people stepped on her feelings.

But not Arthur. Arthur made her feel interesting and lovely and popular.

Piney's show lasted a long time. After his last song, Tina approached the stage. "You were really good," she said to him.

It was one-fifteen in the morning and Piney looked beat. But he looked happy, too. "Everybody seemed to like the show. That makes me feel good."

As they walked to the van, Tina said, "A guy asked me out tonight."

He turned and stared at her. "Yeah?"

"Yeah. A real classy guy. His parents own a quarter horse ranch. He asked me out and I said okay."

Piney shrugged his shoulders. "If you want to."

"I told him some stuff about me that wasn't true. He thinks I come from a nice rich family."

Piney laughed. "Susie, that wasn't too smart."

"What do you mean? It doesn't hurt anything. But the truth sure would," Tina said as she climbed into the van.

"What happens if he gets to liking you? You'll have to tell him you lied then."

"So what? He'll understand. He seems like a real nice guy."

Piney laughed. "You an expert on guys?" The way he laughed seemed to say he thought Tina had never had a date in her life.

"I've been out with plenty of guys," Tina snapped. "I can tell from a guy's eyes what he's like inside."

"What about my eyes, Susie?"

"What?"

"Well, you said you could tell. What am I like on the inside?" He grinned at her.

Tina glared back. Maybe if Piney weren't such an arrogant person, she would like him—like him a lot. But he didn't take her seriously. He didn't realize she was a lot more grown-up than he thought. Piney felt sorry for her, but that was all—or at least that was how he acted.

The next night at The Century Plant, a lovely girl came and sat in the front. She wore beautiful, fashionable clothes. Her dark, thickly lashed eyes widened when Piney stepped out on stage. She stared directly at him.

Piney saw her, too. He sang to her all night.

They say the eyes are windows to the soul,
that eyes are the key to a locked heart.
Well, if that's true, then tell me, lady,
why such sweet eyes tore my life apart.

Tina stared at Piney as he smiled at the admiring girl. She was angry. She knew it was stupid to feel angry. She didn't own Piney. He wasn't her boyfriend, and it was foolish to believe he ever would be. Still, Tina felt angry.

Piney went on singing and looking into the girl's big eyes.

They say the eyes will tell what's true,
even when the smile is a painted lie.
They say the eyes are windows to the
*   soul,*
that the deepest pain is in tears you
*   cry.*

It may be true, sweet lady, and yet
those eyes of yours burned out a hole,
left me dying, left me wondering
if the devil made those windows to
*   your soul.*

The girl in the front row almost fell out of her chair applauding.

Later when Piney took a break, he came down and had a drink with her. Sitting nearby, Tina could hear most of their conversation.

"If you ain't the most exciting singer," the girl said.

"Aw, go on, honey," Piney said.

"I'm country, too. I was born in Tennessee." The girl's voice was gooey like wet sugar.

"Yeah? No kidding?"

"Nashville, honey. Sure enough, Nashville, Tennessee." Then she laughed. "You're so sweet, Piney. Sweeter than sweet potato pie."

"You're pretty sweet yourself," Piney said. Tina thought he sounded like a big fool.

"Bet you got girls drooling all over you clear to Alaska," the girl said.

"None of them as pretty as you, honey," Piney said.

She shoved him playfully and he grabbed her. He pulled her onto his lap. She sat there like a big empty-headed doll.

The sight made Tina sick to her stomach. She hurriedly got up and went into the kitchen to help make French fries.

In a few minutes Piney came into the kitchen, too. He looked around, then asked, "You seen Tuba around, Susie?"

"No," she replied coldly. Then she got a whiff of his breath. "You smell like a wino."

"Come on, Susie, I had one drink.

What's the matter with you? You look at me like I'm some kind of disease."

Tina chopped at the potatoes. "I never saw you drunk before."

"Drunk! I'm not drunk." Then Piney began to smile. "I know what's the matter with you. You're jealous."

"Jealous?" Tina exclaimed. She laughed. "Jealous of you and your little fan? You think I care if you make a fool of yourself?"

He was grinning. "Yeah, I do. You're jealous."

Tina grabbed a towel and threw it at Piney. He caught it, laughing. Then he went back to the stage.

Tina closed her eyes and took a deep breath. She tried to think about Arthur. Arthur liked her, didn't he? He'd asked her out. Friday, she would have a good time with a nice, classy guy. What did it matter if Piney started chasing some wide-eyed fan?

Tina blinked hard. There was a tear in her eye.

"Damn!" she said bitterly. She'd cut her finger on the chopping knife.

5 PINEY WENT OUT with his new girlfriend that night. He didn't get back to the van until three in the morning. When he crept into the van, Tina pretended she was asleep, but she wasn't.

On Thursday, Tina bought a cheap blue dress and matching shoes with her baby-sitting money and wages.

She showed off the outfit for Piney. As she turned in a circle, the dress swirled around her knees in a pretty way.

Piney whistled. "Not bad, Susie."

"You're making fun of me," she said.

He laughed. "Am not."

Tina studied him. She couldn't tell what he was really thinking. She told herself she was stupid to be wondering at all. Piney Woods was nothing to her. He would never be anything to her. It was Arthur she should be thinking about.

On Friday, Arthur arrived at seven. They drove south into the valley. First they went to a movie that Tina didn't understand. Then they went to a restaurant.

It was the finest restaurant Tina had ever seen. She had never dreamed of eating in such a nice place. Yet though she was thrilled to be in the elegant restaurant, Tina was on edge. She feared she'd say something crude or stupid that would give herself away.

Arthur handed Tina the menu. Most of the food was described in a foreign language.

"Have you been here before, Arthur?" she asked.

"Sure."

"Then you surprise me and order the best thing on the menu. I'll bet you're a regular *gourmet*." Tina was glad she had remembered one word from all those vocabulary lists in school.

Arthur smiled. "I do enjoy good food."

The waiter brought duck with orange sauce and a salad. Everything was marvelous. The meal ended with chocolate mousse.

Tina had never tasted such good food in her life. However, she pretended it was all very routine. She had to keep reminding herself that Arthur thought she was rich, too.

As they left the restaurant, Tina said, "It was lovely, Arthur. Everything was perfect." She hoped "lovely" was the right word. It sounded classy, didn't it?

"I'm glad you enjoyed it."

"Oh, I did."

"I enjoyed being with you, Tina," Arthur said as he opened the car door for her. "In fact, I'd like to see you again. We're having this dance at my college fraternity next week. Would you be able to go with me?"

"Sounds great," Tina said.

"Wonderful." Arthur pulled away from the curb and said, "You know, Tina, I can't wait for my folks to meet you either. We're having an informal barbecue on Sunday. Nothing fancy—just the family. Could you come?"

"This Sunday?" Tina asked.

"If you have other plans—" Arthur looked disappointed.

Tina's heart was pounding. She didn't want to turn Arthur down. But she dreaded the thought of meeting his parents. It probably wouldn't take them long to figure out that she was only pretending to be rich. That would ruin everything.

But Arthur looked so disappointed that Tina smiled and said, "Sunday is fine."

Tina told Piney about her plans for Sunday. "Arthur really likes me," she said. "I can't see why. Nobody like him ever looked at me before."

"You better tell him the truth, Susie," Piney warned.

Tina ignored that. "His folks have horses. I hope he doesn't want me to ride. I told him I could ride. Is it hard to ride a horse?"

Piney laughed. "Just get up there and hang on tight."

Tina worried a lot about Sunday. On Saturday, she sat in The Century Plant watching Piney practice. He had just written a new song and Tina listened to the words.

Some days are bad, and others are

worse,
some days are a sorrow, and others a
*   curse.*
The day I left home, I was chasing a lie,
looking for true love 'fore I died.

The day I met you was a dream come
*   true,*
but your poisoned lips soon chilled me
*   blue.*
And now that I'm broken and busted
*   as well,*
my life's all over and there's nothing
*   to tell.*

Just write on my tombstone when I'm
*   cold and alone*
that here lies a man who was cut to the
*   bone.*
Learn from my story, and weep if you
*   can.*
Just write on my tombstone, this once
*   was a man.*

Tina felt even more depressed after she
heard Piney's song. She went to bed, but

she couldn't sleep. Tomorrow was Sunday and her date with Arthur.

However, when the next day came, the date seemed to get off to a smooth start. Arthur was in a good mood when he came. He smiled warmly when he saw Tina. Tina tried to smile back.

Arthur drove her to his family's ranch. The place seemed enormous to Tina. There were redwood fences, green pastures, and beautiful horses everywhere.

Arthur's father, a big well-built man, gave Tina a pleasant welcome. He truly seemed to like Tina. He called her a "right pretty little gal."

But Arthur's mother was different. Tina knew right away that she would have a hard time fooling Mrs. Morley. She was a slim, good-looking woman, except for her piercing little eyes. Those eyes were like a hawk's, the kind that can turn you inside out.

"So you're from Arkansas, are you, dear?" Mrs. Morley said. "We have friends in Little Rock. Perhaps you know them: Roy and Cora Jackson?''

"No—no, I don't believe I know that name." Tina was shaking inside. She hoped she wasn't shaking on the outside, too.

"Your accent is different from the Jacksons'," Mrs. Morley went on. "Seems odd."

"I guess I've lost my Arkansas accent," Tina said. She felt like she was slipping into a deep hole. She kept remembering something her mother had once said: *Nice guys never take me out, sweetie. I guess I got a sign on me or something.*

Tina felt that, like her mother, she was wearing a sign. And like her mother, she didn't belong with classy people—people like Arthur. It had been a mistake to go out with him in the first place. The more she thought about it, the more convinced Tina became that this day would end badly.

"Want to go riding, Tina?" Arthur said.

"What?" Tina turned her head sharply.

"Riding. I thought we'd take a nice ride

before we eat Dad's steaks," Arthur said.

"Good idea," Mrs. Morley said. "I bet you haven't ridden a horse since you left Arkansas, have you, Tina?" She had a strange gleam in her eye. Tina was afraid Arthur's mother had her figured out already. She'd probably guessed Tina's folks didn't own any ranch in Arkansas.

But Tina was trapped. If she was wearing a sign, it must say "liar," she thought grimly.

Mr. Morley excused himself to look after the barbecue, and they walked to the horse corral. To Tina, the animals looked like monsters. They snorted and paced wildly around the pen.

Tina stared at the horses. She imagined what might happen to her if she actually tried to ride one of these animals. She could easily be thrown—even stomped on.

"Pick me a gentle horse, Arthur," Tina said.

"Sure will. Here's a little filly that the neighbor kid rides." He led a black horse over.

Mrs. Morley sat on the corral fence and

watched. "Do you want to bridle her yourself, Tina? You look to me like the kind of girl who would want to bridle her own horse."

Arthur handed Tina a tangle of leather straps. She stared at the mess. The straps were going in all directions. She didn't even know where to begin.

"Uh—Arthur—would you bridle the horse for me? My brothers always did it at home."

"Oh, sure," he said.

When it was time to mount the horse, Tina wasn't sure how to do that, either. A leather thing hung at the side of the horse. Tina figured that was the stirrup. She'd seen cowboys in the movies step into one when they mounted up.

Tina hesitantly stepped into the stirrup. But just then the horse moved. Tina fell backwards into the dirt.

Mrs. Morley climbed down from the fence and walked over to Tina. Her face was cold and angry. "You've never ridden a horse in your life, have you?"

Tina stared at Arthur. "I—I'm sorry.

I just told you I rode horses to please you." She knew she was caught.

"And there is no ranch in Arkansas, is there?" Mrs. Morley demanded. Her voice was as tense as a bowstring.

Tina's lips began to tremble. "I—I just wanted to please Arthur."

Arthur stared at Tina. "Was everything a lie?" Tina couldn't stand to meet his eyes. He looked like a kid who'd just lost a treasured autographed baseball. She didn't know what made her feel worse—Arthur's hurt look or Mrs. Morley's fiery glare.

"I guess I'd better go home," Tina said.

"I think you'd better," Mrs. Morley coldly agreed.

Tina followed Arthur to his car. He didn't speak a word until the car was in motion. Then he said, "You sure made a fool out of me."

"Oh, Arthur, I just wanted you to like me."

He closed his mouth grimly.

After a minute, he said angrily, "I'll bet that Piney Woods isn't even your brother."

"He's like my brother," Tina said softly.

Arthur turned and stared at Tina. "You're staying with him and he isn't your brother. You're just—" He swallowed. His face was tense and furious.

He didn't have to finish. Tina knew what he was thinking. She felt icy cold inside, but all she could say was, "I'm sorry."

They didn't talk anymore. Arthur dropped her off at The Century Plant. Then he drove away as fast as he could. His tires squealed as he vanished around a corner.

Piney had seen the whole thing. He shook his head. "I told you to tell him the truth."

"Oh, shut up!" Tina snapped.

"Susie, Susie, I warned you—"

"I don't need him!" Tina shouted. "I don't need anybody. And you can stop calling me Susie! You can stop calling me anything! I don't need anybody, including you. I never had a living soul care about me, and I'm doing just fine! So leave me alone!"

"Come on, kid, don't be stupid," Piney said.

"I said leave me alone!" Tina went inside the van and slammed the door. Piney didn't follow her. He had a show to do.

Tina counted her money. She only had a few dollars left. She'd spent all the rest on that stupid dress.

She stared at Piney's bag. In the distance, she could hear him singing for the crowd in The Century Plant.

She made up her mind. Hurriedly she rummaged through the bag and found Piney's wallet. Twenty dollars. That's all she'd take. She stuffed the money into her big straw bag. She promised herself that she'd pay Piney back after she got to L.A. and found a job.

Tina got out of the van and started towards the highway. She could still hear Piney's voice drifting down on the night wind.

—and thank you, Lord, for all my

friends,
who never try to tie down my wings.

It was funny, Tina thought. That was the first song she'd heard him sing that night in Albuquerque. And it would be the last song she'd ever hear him sing.

Tina rubbed the tears from her cheeks. It was stupid to cry. What good would crying do? If crying helped anything, then her mother might love her a little or at least drink less.

Tina saw the headlights of a car coming down the highway. She jerked out her thumb. The lights of the car caught her as it rushed past.

Then the car slowed down and backed up. Tina ran towards it. She knew it was going south, toward L.A.

She hoped the driver wasn't another Jack or even another Piney. All she wanted was a ride to L.A.—a place to lose herself and forget.

6 THE DRIVER TURNED out to be a middle-aged businessman. He was on his way to Long Beach and said he'd welcome the company to stay awake.

"So you're in college, huh?" The man smiled. Tina had told him she was heading back to school after a weekend at home. She'd become an expert at lying.

"Yeah."

"What college do you go to?"

"Northridge. The one in Northridge."

"Well! What a coincidence. My daughter graduated from there. She was on the newspaper staff. Say, why don't I cut off the freeway and drop you right at the college?"

"I don't want to inconvenience you," Tina protested.

"Listen, it's late. I'd hate to think of my daughter having to make a long walk at this time of night. Do you live in the dorms?"

"No. No, I live in a house with a couple of other girls."

"Sorority house, huh?"

"Uh-huh."

They talked about other things until they reached Northridge. Then as he neared the college, he asked, "What street do you live on?"

Tina froze. She didn't know the names of the streets. "You turn right at the next corner," she said quickly. She saw a large building two blocks away. She thought it was probably part of the college. Some of the buildings on the street had Greek letters on them. Tina figured those were the sorority houses.

He turned and drove slowly. Tina said, "That house with the green roof."

He stopped at the curb. "Can you get in all right?"

"Sure," Tina smiled at him, "and thanks so much."

As he drove away, Tina walked up to the door. She watched and waited until the car turned the corner. Then she headed back toward the street.

Just then a voice from inside the house stopped her. "You looking for somebody?" Tina turned and saw a girl leaning out from a window.

"Brenda," Tina said without thinking.

"No Brenda here. You sure you got the right house?"

"Maybe not," Tina said.

The girl looked understanding. "Hey, you need a place to sleep tonight?"

"Uh, yeah. Yeah, I do."

"Okay, go down three houses. It's a pink stucco. Tell them Margo sent you."

"Thanks," Tina said. She hurried down the street to the pink stucco and rapped on the door. A thin girl let her in when she mentioned Margo's name.

Four sleeping bags lay on the floor in the front room, but only two were occupied. Tina found a corner and curled up. She was asleep in five minutes.

The next morning, Tina was awakened by the smell of strong coffee. She got up and followed the odor into the kitchen. There she found the thin girl making breakfast.

The girl looked up. "Morning. I'm Lori."

Tina blinked the sleep from her eyes.

"I'm Tina. Hey, thanks for letting me stay last night."

Lori smiled. "No trouble. Want some corn flakes?"

"Sure."

"Bathroom's down the hall."

Tina went to the bathroom and tied back her long, brown hair. She washed her face and felt a little better. The bruise around her eye was beginning to fade.

She returned to the kitchen and found Lori sitting with two other girls. After greeting one another, they sat down and began eating.

"Do all of you go to school?" Tina asked.

Lori nodded. "Yeah. We work, too."

"I sure need a job," Tina said.

"I work for a guy. He always needs kids," Lori said. "It's modeling. Not big money, but okay for a student. We all work for him."

Tina looked at the girls. They were skinny and pretty. She was skinny, too, but not nearly as pretty as they were. "I don't think he'd want me."

"Don't be silly," Lori said. "Come with me this morning, and I guarantee you a job. And you'd be doing me a favor. The guy gives me ten bucks for every new model I can find."

"Are you kidding?" Tina asked.

"No, I'm not. Finish up your breakfast and I'll prove it to you."

Tina hurriedly did so. After changing her clothes, she followed Lori to a small sports car that had seen better days. They drove about two miles to an old two-story house. The grass had long since disappeared from the lawn area. The only living things in the yard were two ancient palm trees.

Tina wore her blue dress. It was the best thing she had. She'd read once that some models got to keep the dresses they modeled. She hoped that was true.

Inside the house she found three men in the living room, two young and one middle-aged. One of the young men stood up and smiled at Lori. "Hi, baby. Hey, you got me a new model?"

"Yeah," Lori said. "This is Tina."

"Hello, Tina." The man grinned. "I'm Alex. So you want to make some money? It's good pay for short hours."

Alex peeled some bills off a roll of money and gave them to Tina. It seemed like a lot. "This is an advance. It means I'm taking a chance."

"I—I've never modeled before," Tina said. "You understand that, don't you?"

He laughed. "Sure, I understand. Well, come on, Tina. We haven't got all day."

Tina put the money in her straw bag and followed Alex down a long hallway to a small room. Apart from the photographic equipment, the only things in the room were a couch and two chairs.

Tina wondered where the new clothes were. Surely they didn't want to take pictures of her in this cheap blue dress.

"I hope this dress is okay," Tina said.

Alex threw back his head and laughed. Tina watched as he adjusted the lights and the camera. Then he said, "Anytime you want, honey."

"What?"

"Come on, kid. I'm ready to start

shooting. That's what we're here for, right?"

"Where do you want me to stand? I've never done anything like this before. I did a fashion show in school once, but—"

Alex smiled in a funny way. "Lori told you what this was all about, didn't she?"

Tina stared at him.

"Honey, you don't think I'm putting you on the cover of a big fashion magazine, do you? You're not exactly Helen of Troy, you know. You're a fresh-looking kid, and I'm doing a nice little magazine for adults. So are you interested or not? I haven't got all day."

With shaking hands, Tina reached into her bag and took out the money that Alex had given her. She put it down on one of the chairs and walked to the door. Alex's laugh echoed behind her as she fled down the hall.

Tina let herself out of the house and hurried down the street. She stopped at the corner and reached into her bag. She had to see just how much money she had left.

Sudden blinding tears stung her eyes. The money she'd taken from Piney was gone! Somebody must have robbed her last night. Now she had only a few dollars left!

Desperate, Tina headed for a major intersection and then hitched a ride into Hollywood. She went from one restaurant to the next looking for a waitressing job.

After a while Tina grew discouraged. Most of the places didn't want anybody. A few people looked suspicious and said they didn't hire runaway kids.

Finally one very dirty-looking man in a diner said he'd take her on a trial basis.

"We'll see if you work out," he said.

Around three that afternoon, a man in his early thirties came in and ordered a drink. He looked closely at Tina. "You're new here."

"Yeah."

"Well, I'm Eddie." He paused and then leaned closer. "Say, if you get sick of working here, I could use you."

"What kind of work?" Tina asked.

"Oh, I buy stuff you might run across."

He smirked at her.

"I've got nothing to sell you," Tina said.

Eddie smirked again. "You might find something. For instance, let's say you find a watch. You know, maybe you find it just laying there in the street. Bring it to me and I'll buy it."

"You want me to steal for you," Tina said.

"Steal? Nobody said anything about stealing." His smile wouldn't quit. He finished his drink in silence. As he dumped a tip on the table, he added, "If you need me, I'm at the pool hall on the corner."

Tina did all right in the diner when the customers came slowly. But when the diner filled up around six, she began to make mistakes. She brought the wrong orders and mixed up salad dressings. She gave somebody whipped cream on his pie when he didn't order it. He refused to pay for it, but he ate it anyway.

The dirty-looking owner yelled at Tina. The more he yelled, the more mistakes she made. Finally she got so nervous she dropped a full pot of coffee.

"That's it, kid," the owner shouted. "Beat it!"

He gave Tina a couple of dollars. That, plus her tips, came to a grand total of five dollars.

Tina wandered out onto the street. It was seven-thirty and it was getting dark. The street was filling up with strange-looking people.

Tina looked around. She was frightened. She didn't have enough money for a room—scarcely enough for a meal.

Then she spotted a pay phone. She stared for a moment, then hurried to the booth. Piney; maybe Piney would forgive her. Maybe he would let her come back. She trembled as she dialed The Century Plant.

But it was Tuba who answered the phone. And he knew her voice. "Hey, you the thief who ripped his money off? Listen, you can go to jail—"

Tina hung up quickly. Piney was probably furious at her. He might have even reported her to the police. She couldn't go back there.

She thought for a minute. Then she put more money in the phone and dialed her mother.

"Mom?" Tina could barely keep her voice from shaking.

"Sweetie, is that you?" This time her mother didn't sound like she'd been drinking.

"Yeah, Mom, listen—"

"Honey, I'm married!" her mother cried.

Tina swallowed hard. "Married?"

"Harry really married me. I never thought he would. I'm happy as a kid. Listen, you got to come visit—uh, later on, you understand. Not right away. You know how you and Harry didn't hit it off. I mean, I wouldn't want to get him mad. But later on, you got to come visit."

Tina felt abandoned, like a little kid who'd suddenly lost her parents in a great crowd of people.

"Well, how's it going with you, honey? I bet you're doing fine, hey? You always had plenty of grit."

"I'm okay, Mom."

"Got a guy, huh?"

"Uh, yeah."

"Good for you. Listen, Tina, you come visit. Okay?"

"Sure."

"Got to hang up now. Harry's here. Glad you called."

"Goodbye, Mom," Tina whispered.

Tina had known it before she called. There was no home for her to go back to.

Tina remembered something her mother had once said.

Tina, you probably can't understand this, but you've got to try. See, I didn't want a baby. I was just a kid myself. And you weren't just a doll I could play with and then put away when I got tired. You were a real kid, and you screamed and cried. I didn't need it or want it.

Her mother had been wrong. Tina did understand—kind of. She knew her mother loved her. But she also knew that her mother had had a hard time bringing up a kid by herself.

Tina's father—he hadn't even known her mother was pregnant. Just another one of those men who had drifted into her mother's life and quickly gone. Leaving her mother alone and still looking for someone to love her—someone other than Tina.

Tina stood on the dark street and thought about Piney's song: *Please don't ask me to love you, that's something I just can't do.* He'd said it for everybody.

Tina wondered why she'd even been born. Who needed her?

It was getting cold on the street. Tina looked around desperately. Where could she go?

Then she saw the jewelry store. Slowly, almost unwillingly, Tina walked towards it. With a sudden plunge, she pushed open the door.

The clerk was busy with a woman. Nervously, Tina watched him out of the corner of her eye. Then she grabbed four watches with trembling hands and stuffed them frantically into her straw bag. Her heart was beating so fast that she felt sick. But nobody stopped her when she walked out the door.

Once she was out of sight of the store, she slowed down. She didn't want to go through with the rest of this. But it was too late now. And she had to have the money.

Eddie grinned when he saw her.

"I knew you'd come through," he said. "I can always spot them."

He gave Tina some money for the watches. "First time is always the roughest," he said. "Next time it'll be a lot easier."

"There won't be a next time," Tina said. And she told herself she was going to pay for the watches. She would mail the money back to the jewelry store as soon as she could.

"Sure, sure," Eddie grinned. He winked.

Tina swallowed hard. She'd come to L.A. to lose herself. Well, she'd done it all right. She wondered if she could ever find her way back.

7 TINA GOT A room in a hotel. It had a private bath and old, musty furniture. She lay down on the faded bedspread and cried herself to sleep.

The next day Tina tried to get another job. Most of the places turned her down cold. One man in a taco stand told her to wait while he asked his wife. Then he went into the back and Tina heard him say to his wife, "I think she's a runaway. I'm going to stall her. You call the cops."

That was all Tina needed to hear. She took off at once.

Up and down the streets she went. Yet nowhere could she find a job.

Around six, she ran into Eddie. Tina started to walk right past him, but he caught her arm. "Hey, wait a minute. I'm going to a nice place for a steak dinner. Want to come along? It's on me."

"No."

"Listen. No strings. Just a steak dinner."

Tina shrugged. She was hungry and didn't have that much money anyway.

She got in his car and they drove about two miles to a nice restaurant.

As they ate their meal, Eddie said, "Tell me about yourself, kid."

"Nothing to tell. I ran away from home."

"Your folks looking for you?"

Tina shook her head.

"Great. Listen, I got a little rental in North Hollywood. You could stay there while we work something out."

"I don't want to stay with you," Tina said coldly.

"Wouldn't be staying with me. It's an empty apartment. Look, I got this really sweet deal in mind that might be good for both of us."

"I can't steal stuff. That last time almost killed me," Tina said.

Eddie put down his knife and fork and leaned across the table. "Look, honey, it wouldn't be like that. See, I got a new deal going. I got a friend in an employment agency. This agency lines up household help for rich people. I recruit the housekeepers and baby-sitters and stuff. Give them phony letters of reference. Then they tell me when the coast is clear. I go in, pick up a few valuables. They're in the clear." Eddie shrugged his shoulders matter-of-factly and began eating again.

Tina shook her head. "I can't do stuff like that. I'm going to pay back what I already took."

"Okay, listen. How about I just show you the apartment? Then if you want to, you can rent it," Eddie said.

"I guess so," Tina agreed. She was too weary to argue.

Eddie drove Tina to the apartment and showed her around. Then he said he'd come back in the morning and they would talk.

After he left, Tina sat in a chair in the dark. She felt totally hopeless, as though she were sinking into quicksand. The more she stole for Eddie, the deeper she would sink.

Then someday they would catch her. That would mean jail. Maybe it wouldn't happen right away. But sooner or later—

Tina shuddered. She could hear the prison doors clanging shut. No light, no air—no future. What was the point?

Tina got to her feet and went into the bathroom. Searching through her straw bag, she found it—the bottle of aspirin. She emptied the whole bottle into the palm of her hand. She didn't know how many aspirins there were, but the bottle was almost full.

Tina filled a paper cup with water. She felt her body tighten, and sweat began to pour down her face. She squeezed her eyes shut and tried to take a mouthful of the tablets.

But she couldn't do it. She threw the tablets in the sink and dropped, sobbing, onto the floor.

Tina cried for a long time. Finally she was too tired to cry any longer. She got up and washed her face. Then she staggered off to bed. She fell into a restless sleep.

That night she dreamed of Piney Woods. She imagined Piney was a world-famous singer, performing in front of thousands of cheering, clapping people. As he sang, Piney twirled his guitar. It shot beams of rainbow-colored light into the audience.

The crowd grew wilder. They jumped up on chairs and screamed.

Suddenly a hush fell over the crowd. Piney was calling somebody onto the stage. At first Tina didn't hear the name. But then the crowd took up the name and chanted it.

"Ti-na, Ti-na," they chanted.

Stunned, Tina slowly got up from her seat. She walked down the aisle into the blinding stage lights. Piney stood there in a shining coat, his arms open. Tina walked right into his arms, and everybody clapped.

Tina woke up. The dream told her what she hadn't wanted to face: she loved Piney Woods. Maybe she had known it from the beginning. It was so hopeless and silly. But she couldn't hide the truth any longer.

Tina slowly crawled out of bed. Her face felt stiff from crying. Her eyes stung when she looked at the rays of sun coming through the broken blinds.

After she washed and dressed, Tina put twenty dollars in an envelope. She addressed it to Piney, care of The Century Plant. At least she'd paid him back now. It made her feel a little better.

Eddie showed up at nine. He was dressed in a nice suit and looked just like an ordinary businessman.

"Did you sleep okay, honey?" he asked pleasantly.

"Yeah."

"Great. Look, I want to tell you about this job. You just listen. If you don't like the sound of it, fine, okay.

"See, there's this family in Encino. The guy has a fantastic coin collection and some pricey pieces of art. Anyway, they need a companion for their daughter. She's sick or something. My friend at the employment agency will send you out today. I've even got letters fixed up saying you've had a year of college."

"It makes me sick," Tina said.

Eddie calmly ignored her comment.

"The family's name is Lovell. Just the husband, wife, and kid. You could work there a few weeks, you know. You know, put me onto the good stuff. Then find out when the family's gone.

"Nobody'd blame you. I'd tie you up the night I robbed the place. They'd feel sorry for you. And you get twenty-five percent of the action." Eddie grinned.

"I can't," Tina said.

"Honey, these people are rich. All the stuff is insured. You wouldn't be hurting anybody. Look, kid, everybody steals. The government steals, the big companies steal—"

"No. I won't do it!" Tina shouted.

Eddie shrugged his shoulders. "Okay, okay. Have it your way. But look, kid, you need a job. So let's say I get you hooked up with them anyway. I'll give you the phony letters, make you look good. You get a nice job. No sweat. If you change your mind about working with me, then I'm ahead. How about that, honey?" Eddie was still smiling.

Tina didn't trust him. But she needed

a job desperately. "I guess that's okay."

"Beautiful," he said.

Tina changed into her blue dress and pulled her hair back with a clasp. Eddie said she looked perfect. He gave her some impressive letters. They said that Tina Hayes had attended one year of college in Boston. The letters also reported that she'd been a volunteer for a children's social work program.

"I won't help you steal from those people," Tina said. "But if I get the job, I'll give you half of my first paycheck."

"That's fair," Eddie agreed.

Tina knew that Eddie was just playing along with her. He thought she'd feel so obligated to him that she'd help him steal.

Well, he was wrong. Tina was going to pay the jewelry store *and* Eddie when she got her first paycheck. Then she'd be in the clear.

Eddie drove Tina to the Lovells. It was a huge, beautiful house.

Tina went in alone. Mr. Lovell met her at the door. He was a stocky, pleasant-looking, middle-aged man. He smiled when he saw Tina. "You must be Tina Hayes."

Tina smiled nervously in return. "Yes."

"Well, I'm Michael Lovell," he said. "The employment agency said you come highly recommended."

Tina handed him the letters and he skimmed them. He seemed very pleased by the information. No wonder; Eddie lied even better than Tina.

Mr. Lovell led Tina into a living room that looked like the cover of a Sunday magazine. Everything was rich and tasteful.

"My wife will be down in a minute," Mr. Lovell said. "First, Tina, I'd like to tell you about our daughter, Linda. She was a sophmore in high school when she began to get sick. She eventually had to drop out of school and be tutored at home.

"Linda is no complainer. But we know she gets lonely without kids her own age. We need someone to be like a sister to her. And someone who can coax her into taking it easy when she should."

Mr. Lovell's voice shook a little, and he paused for a moment. "Linda tends to forget sometimes that she's sick. She just puts so much of herself into her work. You see, Linda's been working with emotionally disturbed children for a long time now. She did wonders with those kids— she still does. But she gets tired quickly now." He cleared his throat and Tina looked down.

"I understand you've worked with children, too," he continued.

Tina felt as though her mouth were filled with sawdust. "Oh, yes. I love kids."

"That's the main thing," Mr. Lovell said. Then he told Tina about the salary, which sounded very good. He also explained that Tina would live with them.

"In a way, what I'm asking is that you become part of our family, Tina. Do you think that would appeal to you?" Mr. Lovell asked.

"Yes—yes I do," Tina said.

It all sounded too good to be true. Tina

was used to not trusting people and having them not trust her in return. She found it hard to believe: someone trusted, liked, and even needed her.

Mrs. Lovell came in then. She was a small, friendly woman. She reminded Tina of a tiny, beautiful bird. Tina liked her right away.

After greeting one another, Mrs. Lovell said, "I think you should meet Linda now."

Tina followed Mrs. Lovell up the wide, carpeted stairs. At the top of the steps, she turned. A look of gentle sadness came over her face. "Tina, do you understand that Linda is very sick?"

Tina felt numb. "Yes—yes, Mr. Lovell told me. She had to quit school?"

"That's right. But you see, Linda doesn't know how sick she is. She believes she's getting better."

Tina didn't know what to say. Mrs. Lovell's words made her feel empty inside. She wanted to turn around and flee this house.

"Maybe she *is* getting better," Tina

finally said.

Mrs. Lovell didn't reply. She just led Tina to a room at the end of the hall and opened the door.

Tina entered. There on the floor she saw a young, thin girl cutting paper daisies from yellow paper. The girl was sitting cross-legged in a mountain of paper.

She grinned when she saw Tina. "Hi. You must be Tina. I'm Linda. Grab some scissors and pitch in."

Tina walked into the room and stood awkwardly next to Linda.

"There's a birthday party for Tommy tomorrow and I have to finish these daisies," Linda explained. "Tommy is a little boy at a special school." Linda glanced at her mother. "Did you tell Tina about the school, Mom?"

"Your father did," Tina jumped in.

"Well, I'll let you two get acquainted," said Mrs. Lovell.

After Mrs. Lovell had left, Tina felt a little less ill at ease. She sat down beside Linda and began cutting out daisies.

Linda smiled in encouragement. Then

she said, "Tommy really deserves a great birthday party. He never even smiled when I first came. He sure is smiling now! Tomorrow is his fifth birthday."

Tina soon found herself talking freely to Linda. It was so easy. Tina felt like she'd known Linda all her life. Linda talked and laughed and made Tina feel at home.

Suddenly Linda reached out and grabbed Tina's hands. "Take the job, Tina. *Please*?"

"I want to," Tina said. She'd never wanted anything so much in all her life. She forgot about Eddie. She forgot about how she got the job. All she could think about was how welcome she felt here.

Reality hit her hard in the face when she went downstairs again. There was Eddie, talking to the Lovells. He was telling them how he was an old friend of Tina's family.

Eddie saw Tina and smiled at her. It was an ugly smile to Tina. He looked like a cat licking its whiskers after finishing off a mouse.

Tina felt a sudden chill. The old nightmare was still with her. She hadn't escaped.

8 TINA DID TAKE the job. She couldn't deny she was afraid. Yet she was determined to put Eddie and the stealing behind her.

And the Lovells made it so easy to say yes. When they showed Tina her room, she almost gasped. It was so beautiful. The rug was thick and soft. The four-poster bed had a canopy over it.

The decoration was lovely, too. A seascape on the wall caught Tina's eye. It was an oil painting of silvery water on a sandy beach.

Mrs. Lovell noticed that Tina was staring at the picture. "Linda painted that," she explained.

"Linda!" Tina exclaimed. "She's really talented."

The Lovells offered Tina wonderful comforts. Yet Tina vowed she would give them their money's worth. The very next day, she helped Linda finish the decorations for Tommy's birthday party.

Tina tried to do most of the hard work. She noticed that Linda was much too thin. Sometimes she seemed terribly tired, too. Tina thought that was because she'd been sick for quite a while.

But Linda was getting better, Tina told herself. She refused to believe anything else.

They went to the children's center that afternoon. The Lovells' chauffeur drove them, and the two girls sat in back.

Linda pointed out a few things on the way. Then she said, "Tina, you haven't told me much about your life. What about you?"

Tina laughed, a little embarrassed. "What about me?"

"Well, boyfriends for example. Do you have a regular boyfriend?"

"Sort of," Tina lied.

"I had a nice boyfriend. His name was Chuck," Linda said. "He gave me his school ring. He still comes and visits me sometimes. Usually he's too busy though. He plays football and he's into track, too. What's your boyfriend's name, Tina?"

"Uh—Piney. He's a singer."

"Really? You mean people pay him to sing?"

"Yeah. He makes up his own songs and plays the guitar."

"Are you guys real close?" Linda asked.

"I guess so," Tina said.

"Did he ever kiss you?" Linda asked.

Tina thought she might as well lie again. "Oh, sure."

"I remember the first time Chuck kissed me. He'd never kissed a girl before. It was sort of funny. We were both scared, I think."

She laughed. She was beautiful when she laughed. She didn't even look sick anymore.

"Are you and Piney in love, Tina?"

Tina shrugged. "I'm not sure."

They arrived at the children's center. It was clean and simply furnished. The kids had sad eyes. They looked lonely and afraid. Some of them were very ill.

Looking at the children, Tina understood why few volunteers remained at the center for long. It would be too hard for most people to look at these kids.

But Linda didn't feel that way. As she

laughed and played with the kids, they seemed to come alive. It was clear that they loved Linda and she loved them.

A skinny little boy ran to Linda and hugged her. "This is Tommy, our birthday boy," Linda said.

Earlier, Linda had told Tina about Tommy's history. He had been injured when he was younger. The outside scars had healed. But the ones inside weren't so easy to erase.

Tina understood. She picked Tommy up and held him on her lap. He was shy at first. But when Tina started reading "The Three Bears," Tommy began to smile.

"He likes you," Linda whispered in Tina's ear.

Tina felt an ache inside. It was strange to hear those words. Somebody actually liked her. Okay, so it was only a five-year-old kid. But it was somebody.

Tommy wasn't the only one who seemed to like Tina. When she served the kids the birthday snack, some of them tried to share their treat with her or sit close by.

Linda seemed tired by the end of the party. On the way home she lay her head back on the seat. "You have a way with little kids, Tina," she said.

"You think so?"

"Yes. And I think that's a wonderful gift. They need so much love. You seem to have a lot of love to give." Linda closed her eyes.

Tina felt a strange surge of happiness. Linda's comment made her feel good about herself. That was all too rare for Tina.

The next morning, while Linda was still asleep, Tina took a walk in the Lovells' garden. She was admiring the flowers when a man's voice said, "Hi, honey. How's it going?"

"Eddie!"

"Yeah. Glad you remember me. After all, I'm the nice guy who got you this job." He grinned knowingly.

"Eddie, they paid me in advance for the first month. I want to give you your half," Tina said.

He laughed. "Not so fast, honey. We got a deal."

"I told you I wouldn't steal for you, Eddie."

He sat down on the stone bench. He looked right at Tina. "You like this job, huh?"

"Yeah."

"They think you're a wonderful, sweet kid, right?"

Tina began to tremble. "I guess they like me."

"I wonder what they'd say if they knew the truth about you? What'd they think if they knew you were a runaway? How about if they knew you stole for me?"

"I won't help you rob them," Tina said firmly.

"You think you can sit here with this nice job—a job I got for you? You think you can cut old Eddie out?" He laughed bitterly.

"You blow this deal for me, and I'll blow it for you. I'm not walking away from this empty-handed. There's maybe $40,000 worth of art and coins in that house. Maybe some jewelry, too. I want what you owe me, honey."

"I don't owe you that. I'm not going to let you rob these people. They've been really decent to me, and I won't let you hurt them."

Eddie studied her coldly. His gaze bored into Tina's eyes. "Have you ever been in jail? Do you know what they do to thieves like you?"

"I sent the money back to the jewelry store," Tina said.

"You think that makes a difference? No way, honey, it's not that easy. They'll put you in a cage with mean broads like you never saw before. They'll rip you to pieces, kid." Eddie's voice was mean and hard.

"I don't care."

"I'll tell the cops you're a doper and a thief and any other thing I damn well please. I can make so much trouble for you that you won't believe it."

Tina's heart almost stopped. She turned and looked at Eddie. "Do whatever you want, I still won't help you rob the Lovells. I'll give you half my first paycheck, but that's all I'll give you.''

Eddie glared at Tina. Then he began to laugh in an awful way. "I was going to make you rich, you little fool. The minute I saw you, I knew you and I could work together. I thought—hey, Eddie, that kid has class! She could charm her way into the White House. I figured you and I were a natural team. What a laugh on me.''

Tina's heart was racing. He isn't going to let me off the hook, she thought. He's going to drag me down with him.

Tina didn't know what to do. All she knew for certain was that she wasn't going to help Eddie hurt the Lovells.

9 A LONG, TERRIBLE silence followed. Finally Eddie swore and said, "Give me the lousy money from your pay."

Tina's hands shook as she handed over the money. Eddie grabbed it without a word and walked away. He never once looked back.

Tina couldn't believe he was really gone. She felt as though a great load had been lifted off her shoulders.

Later that day Linda asked Tina if she and Pincy had broken up. "We sort of went in different directions," Tina explained.

"But you still like him, huh?" Linda asked.

Tina flushed. "Maybe."

"Tina, I can tell. You still like him. Listen, why don't you invite him over to the children's center. We're having a big party for a couple of the kids in two weeks. They would really love to hear a singer. They could sing along.

"I'd love it, too. It'd be a great birthday present—I'll be seventeen the same day.''

Tina was torn. She wanted to make Linda happy, and she wanted to see Piney again. But she wasn't sure how Piney felt. Maybe he was still mad at her.

"Well, maybe."

"Oh, Tina, do it! Dad would pay him the same amount he gets for a regular performance."

"Okay, I'll try, Linda."

Linda reached out and hugged Tina. "Oh, you're a doll! If I had a sister, she'd be just like you. *I love you, Tina!*"

The words echoed in Tina's ears. She couldn't remember the last time anybody had said that to her.

Tina hugged Linda back. "I love you too, Linda."

The next day Tina went looking for Piney. The Lovells' chauffeur drove Tina to a small club in North Hollywood. Tina had seen a newspaper ad saying that Piney was appearing there.

She was nervous. She wondered what it would be like to see Piney again. Would he smile and welcome her? Or would he slam the door in her face?

Tina went around to the back of the club and knocked on the door. Piney was probably rehearsing now. A cook opened the door. "Yeah?"

"I'm a friend of Piney Woods. Would you call him for me?" Tina asked in a small, shaky voice.

The cook was gone a few minutes. Then the door opened again. Piney stood there. He didn't smile or show any emotion.

Finally he said, "Well, if it ain't Susie."

"Are you still mad at me?"

"For ripping off my twenty and running off without a word? Naw. Why should that make me mad?" His voice was bitter.

"I sent you the money."

"Yeah."

"Can I come in?" Tina asked.

He backed up and she came inside. "Piney," she said, "I've got a respectable job now."

"Good for you." He still sounded bitter.

"What are you so mad for? I paid you back."

Piney's eyes narrowed. "When I found you and the money gone, I thought you were kidnapped or something. It was a lousy thing you did, girl. How come you didn't leave a note?"

"I didn't think you'd be interested in a note. I didn't think you'd care. After all, what am I to you? You always told me I was a pest."

"Yeah," he said. He seemed very angry.

"I guess I made a mistake coming here," Tina said. She was getting angry now, too. "Maybe I should go."

"What'd you come for anyway?" he snapped. "Something else on your mind, isn't there?"

Tina fought back her own temper. She was doing this for Linda, she reminded herself.

"Yeah, yeah there is. Some rich people hired me to be a kind of companion to this girl. She's sick, Piney. But no matter how sick she is, she's always nice. And thoughtful—she works with handicapped kids, and I help her.

"Anyway, she's giving a party for the kids in two weeks. We wondered if you'd come sing. You'd get paid and everything."

Piney was silent for a long moment. Then he said, "I guess I could make it."

Tina sighed in relief. "That's good. One more thing. It's Linda's birthday. Could you make up a song for her? She's real pretty. Big eyes and soft, shiny hair. She gets a little sad sometimes because she's sick, and I think she'd get a big kick out of a song."

He shrugged. "Why not?"

"Oh—and—" Tina struggled for the words, "I sort of told them I'd had a year of college and came from a nice family."

"Still lying, eh? Okay, I won't blow it for you."

Tina gave him the address and the date. It was all very businesslike. Then she hurriedly left.

During the next two weeks at the children's center, Linda and Tina prepared for the party. Linda got tired quickly. Then Tina would take over and finish the job.

Linda smiled almost all the time, except when she thought nobody was looking. She seemed to be in pain. Tina tried to ignore those signs.

"This is going to be such a great party, Tina," Linda said one afternoon.

"Yeah," Tina said. But she had mixed feelings about it. She really cared about Piney. It would hurt her to see him again and to know that he didn't care about her.

"Tina, the kids at the center love you so much. Listen—if I have to go back to the hospital, you'll keep going to the center, won't you? Those kids, they need somebody who cares for them."

Tina felt a cold wind blow across her heart. "You won't have to go back to the hospital, Linda. You seem like you're getting better all the time to me."

Linda gently shook her head. Then a serious look came over her face. "Tina, we'll always be friends, won't we? No matter what?" There was an urgent note in her voice.

"Sure, always."

"Even if I have to go to the hospital. I mean, whatever happens, we'll always be friends."

There was a tightness in Tina's throat. "Always."

"Whenever something nice happens to you, Tina, I'll know about it. And I'll be glad for you. I'll know, and you'll be able to sense me close by. Even if I'm not right there with you. Tina, I'll always love you. Nothing can change that."

They hugged again. Tina fought back tears.

The day of the party, Piney showed up right on time. He looked terrific, and the kids warmed to him right away. He stood in the middle of the room and sang some simple tunes. The kids sang along and clapped.

Then Piney took a break. He lifted some of the kids on his shoulders, and they screamed in delight.

Tina stared at him. He was so gentle and warmhearted. No wonder she loved him. Everybody did.

Finally Piney made his way to Linda.

"So you're Tina's friend. She told the truth. You *are* beautiful."

Tina could see Linda melt. Then Piney began playing his guitar again. This time he sang just for Linda.

They say there's only one meadow
where the grass is always wet.
They say there's only one mountain
where the sun has never set.

They say that there's an eagle,
who carries the stars on his wings.
They say God, he made an angel,
who sighs like a songbird sings.

Linda's eyes glowed with pleasure. She shone like a brilliant candle glowing in the dark.

Her name is Linda, that angel,
Her love runs as fresh as the dew.
She can conquer any mountain,
She can soar where eagles do.

Her name is Linda, that angel.

Loveliest girl I ever knew.
Loveliest girl I ever knew.

Then Piney bent over and kissed Linda.

The rest of the party was a wonderful success.

After it was all over, Tina walked out to the van with Piney to say goodbye. "You were really great, Piney," she said.

"Thanks."

"Linda was so happy. The kids, too." Tina wanted to say more. She wanted to tell him how she felt. But the words wouldn't come. She wasn't good at telling people she cared. She hadn't had much practice.

Piney waved and drove off. Tina watched him until his van was out of sight. It had been her last chance to tell him how she felt. She'd never have another.

After the party Linda could talk of nothing but Piney. "Oh, Tina, he's so fantastic!"

Despite her excitement, Linda looked drawn and worn-out. It scared Tina.

"You'd better rest now, Linda," she urged. "You've had a lot of excitement today."

Linda did rest for a while. But an hour later she knocked on Tina's door. She still looked so tired that Tina immediately pulled up a chair and insisted that Linda sit down.

Linda looked earnestly at Tina. She said, "Tina, next week is Gina's birthday. You won't forget it, will you?"

Gina was a little redhead at the center. She wore braces on her legs, but bravely joined in all of the games.

"I remember," Tina said. "We should start making decorations."

Linda shook her head. "Tina, not me. Just you. I—I'm not doing well. I think I'll be going back to the hospital."

"Linda—" Tina's mouth went dry. Then she asked quickly, "Have you told your parents how sick you're feeling?"

Linda silently shook her head.

Tina immediately found the Lovells, who called the doctor.

The ride to the hospital was grim and

depressing. Linda was very sleepy from the sedative the doctor had given her.

At the hospital, they quickly wheeled Linda away. Though Tina stayed there until visiting hours were over, she only caught one short glimpse of Linda.

The next day, Tina went to the children's center alone. She read stories to the kids and played with them. Then she went to the hospital to report to Linda.

This time Tina was admitted into the room. Linda was awake and alert. She eagerly questioned Tina, wanting to know everything that had happened.

Day after day, Tina went to see Linda. And day after day, Tina could see her friend was getting weaker. Sometimes Linda didn't even seem to know that Tina was there. She looked less and less like herself, lying in the middle of all the machines.

She went into a coma on a Friday, but the next day she woke up. She seemed happy to see Tina and delighted to hear about the kids. Tina told Linda the kids missed her and she had to get well soon.

That Saturday before she left, Tina bent down and kissed Linda. And that was the last time she saw Linda alive. The next day, at five in the morning, Linda died.

10

TWO WEEKS HAD passed since Linda's death. Much had happened in those weeks. The funeral, the visits to the children's center, long talks with the Lovells. Tina had told the truth about her past during some of those long talks.

Now Mr. Lovell was driving her back to Albuquerque to her mother's.

"You made Linda happier than she ever was," he said. "My wife and I have talked a lot about you, Tina. If you decide not to stay with your mother, we'd like you to come back to us."

He's just being kind, Tina thought. "My mother needs me," she said. "And she's going to be so glad to see me. She made some mistakes, but she's a good mother. She really is."

The house looked the same as it had when she had left. Everything seemed sad and run-down.

Tina began to worry. What if nothing had changed? What if her mother didn't want her?

As she got out of the car, she looked

at Mr. Lovell, then back at the house. "Mr. Lovell, thank you so much for everything."

She expected him to drive away, but he didn't. He said, "I'm going to wait right here until you talk to your mom. If everything is okay and you want to stay, just come to the front window and wave. Then I'll leave."

"Okay," Tina said. "Thanks again, Mr. Lovell." She turned and walked to the front door. She rang the doorbell three times before her mother came to the door.

"Who's there?" her mother called.

"It's me, Mom."

Tina heard something fall. Then she heard her mother opening the door. She prayed everything would be okay.

The front door opened. Tina stared in disappointment at her mother. Her beautiful hair was tangled. Her clothes were stained and rumpled. She'd obviously been drinking.

Tina wanted to cry she felt so sorry for her mother. "Mom," she whispered, opening her arms wide.

"Sweetie, is it really you?"

"Oh, Mom."

But something was wrong. Slowly Tina realized that she was hugging her mother, but her mother wasn't hugging her back. Maybe she'd forgotten how.

They stepped inside and Tina asked, "How are you, Mom?"

"Great—Hey, honey, how—how long you been gone? A couple weeks?"

"Months."

"You missed some school. Hey, Harry and me, we got married. Isn't that something?"

"I know, Mom. It sure is."

Tina's mother walked unsteadily to the kitchen and started to pour herself a drink. She stopped and looked at Tina.

"You don't drink, do you? It's no good for a kid. I won't allow it. You hear me?"

"Yes, Mom," Tina whispered, fighting back tears.

Her mother sat down on the sofa and put her head back. She seemed confused. Tina desperately wanted to tell her that she understood—that she wanted to help her mom, but didn't know how.

At last her mother spoke. "You having a birthday soon. Gonna be what? Sixteen?"

"Seventeen, Mom." Tina was crying. She felt so helpless. It hurt to see her mother like this.

"Harry and me—we had a little fight. But he'll be home soon. Hey, honey, you better not be here when he comes. You know how you two don't get along. Okay?"

"Sure, Mom."

She had to think. She couldn't stay. But first she must send Mr. Lovell away. She couldn't burden him with her problems. She'd wave to him and then wait a minute before leaving.

With her heart breaking, Tina went to the window and waved. Then she quickly closed the curtains. She couldn't bear to look.

She went to the sofa and kissed her mother goodbye.

"Take care, Tina," her mother said. "And you come back and visit soon, all right?"

"Yes."

"And no drinking, okay?"

"No drinking," Tina promised, her voice cracking.

She grabbed her bag and slipped out the door.

She couldn't believe her eyes. Mr. Lovell was standing there, patiently waiting beside his car. He'd known what would happen and he'd waited.

He slowly approached her and gently put his hands on Tina's shoulders. "Tina, come home with me," he urged. "My wife and I need you. For a precious little while we had two fine daughters. Must we lose both of them at once?" Tears welled up in his eyes.

Tina put her arms around him, and they walked back to the car together.

* * *

After a month, it was arranged for Tina to start school again near the Lovell house. She continued going to the children's center.

Then, one Saturday while Tina was

redecorating the bulletin board, a tall figure appeared in the doorway.

"Piney—" Tina gasped.

"How've you been?" Piney asked.

"Okay—I'm in school. I guess maybe someday I'll even go to college." All her old feelings for Piney flooded back into her heart. But she tried to say as calmly as possible, "How's it going for you?"

"I'm keeping busy." He looked at Tina. "You know, we never had a real date, did we?"

"I guess not."

"Are you busy this weekend, Tina?" he asked softly.

"What happened to Susie?" Tina asked.

"I think she grew up." Piney smiled.

"You really want to take me out, Piney?"

"If you don't mind dating a country boy."

Tina smiled. She remembered what Linda once told her:

Whenever something nice happens to

*you, Tina, I'll know about it. And I'll
be glad for you. I'll know, and you'll be
able to sense me close by. Even if I'm
not right there with you.*

"What is it?" Piney asked. He saw a
strange look pass across Tina's face.

"I just felt somebody touching me.
Somebody special."

Piney smiled. He took Tina's hand in
his. It felt good there. It felt very good.